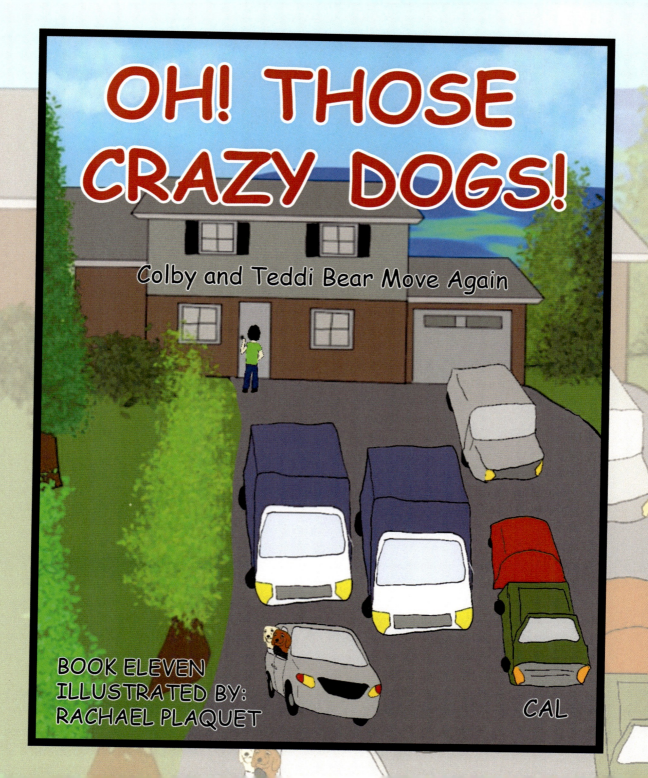

To order additional copies of this book, contact:
Xlibris
844-714-8691
www.Xlibris.com
Orders@Xlibris.com

ISBN: Softcover   979-8-3694-2485-8 (sc)
        EBook   979-8-3694-2484-1 (e)

Library of Congress Control Number: 2024912686

Print information available on the last page

Rev. date: 06/28/2024

OH! THOSE CRAZY DOGS!

Colby and Teddi Bear Move Again

Introduction

This is a story about 2 crazy dogs, their adventures and the mischief they get into.

They are very loving dogs, but they can't help getting into things.

Hi ! I'm Colby! I'm big and red and furry ! I love everyone but sometimes people are afraid of me because I am so big!

Hi ! I'm Teddi Bear! I'm big and white and very furry! I'm not as big as Colby, but just about. Everyone thinks I'm cute and I put shows on for them.

He puts shows on for everyone, rolls on his back and kicks his legs up.

Our owners picked us out specially and brought us home to love and care for us. We love them too, very much. They give us everything and a warm loving home. We will call them Mom and Pop.

Sometimes we don't listen to them, especially me, Teddi Bear!

Our mom and pop love us anyway. Sometimes I get Colby in trouble. I can get him to do anything I want because he loves me too and can't say no. He protects me all the time.

"Colby what are mom and pop doing!" asked Teddi Bear.

"I don't know," replied Colby. "It looks like they're packing some things in boxes. Maybe they just want to put some things away," said Colby.

"Noo... it looks like they are packing to move again," cried Teddi Bear. "No, they can't be. We've only lived here for two years. We can't be moving again!" exclaimed Teddi Bear.

"Let's watch them," said Colby. Both dogs sat and watched mom and pop pack their things into boxes and totes.

"Colby, I think we really are moving again." cried Teddi Bear, "are we not going to have a big yard anymore and a big deck to lay around on and watch the lake?" asked Teddi Bear.

"I don't know" replied Colby. I don't know what their plans are" said Colby, "let's continue watching them and find out." So, Colby and Teddi Bear watched their mom and pop pack up all their belongings again.

They were very sad.

"Where are they bringing us now thought Colby. Colby nudged a box then nudged his mom trying to ask her what was happening. Mom looked down at Colby and said,

"Yes, we are moving again to a smaller property because this one is too big for us to look after. But! Guess what?! We will still have a big yard for you, a bigger house and mama bought you a big pool again! You can swim all the time, except winter, of course!"

"YAY, YAY, YAY" YELLED Colby and Teddi Bear. To mom and pop it just sounded like barking but they could tell the dogs were very happy. Mom and pop continued packing everything while the dogs watched or played outside. They were still worried but mom had reassured them a bit about where they were going.

Finally, the day came when two big trucks and four men arrive at the house. Mom and pop's family showed up with a truck and trailer too. Everyone worked loading up all the stuff. Colby and Teddi Bear could hear things breaking a lot. They were sitting outside with mom to stay out of everyone's way. The loading went on and on until late at night.

Everyone was tired and we still had to drive two hours to get to our new home. Mom's van was filled with boxes and we got into the full van with mom. She drove and drove. We could tell she was tired so we were good boys. Pop had his big van loaded to the top and he was coming after everyone else was finished at the old house so he could lock up, then join us.

Mom started slowing down near some houses then pulled into a large driveway and drove up to a garage. The house was on the side and looked nice but we could smell a pool! A pool! Colby and Teddi Bear were clawing at the door trying to get out of the van.

It was only April and the pool had it's winter cover on but the dogs didn't care. They jumped out of the van as fast as they could, ran past mom, through the garage, over the cement patio and jumped right onto the middle of the cover! It was a safety cover so they just bounced but they were sitting in some water. Both dogs jumped around and splashed in the water. They were so happy they wouldn't come out when mom called them. Colby and Teddi Bear just sat and soaked in the pool so mom let them stay there because they were safe in the fenced yard and wouldn't interfere with the movers unloading the furniture.

It was very, very late when the movers finished. Colby and Teddi Bear were soaking wet and mom called the dogs in for pop to towel dry them off.

"Hey, this place is different!" said Colby.

"Yeah, I like it though" said Teddi Bear." "Wow this is a big kitchen!

All the rooms are big here. They both galloped up the stairs. Look at all the rooms up here! Little rooms and very big rooms.

"Wow! I like it!", exclaimed Teddi Bear. "It's so different from what we had before. And it has a big yard for us to play in and a pool for us! This is awesome!"

Colby and Teddi Bear were so happy with their new home. They had lots of room to run inside and outside except the living and dining rooms. They had to be careful there. Both of their beds were placed in mom's bedroom and there was still lots of space for them to move around in. All the people left and we went to bed. Poor Colby and Teddi Bear had such a long rough day.

The next morning Teddi Bear and Colby got up and looked out the patio door.

"Hey" said Teddi Bear, all we can see is a deck and a fence. We can't see the pool from here! What's going on? Where is it? Mom came and opened the patio door for us and we bounded outside! We ran around the corner of the house and there it was!

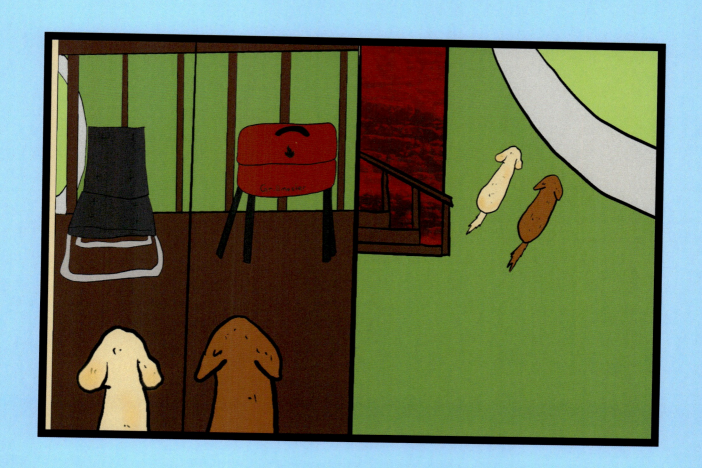

Colby and Teddi Bear ran and jumped right onto the winter cover which had water on it. "Hey!" exclaimed Teddi Bear "this cover thing is still on! We still can't swim."

"It's still early spring" said Colby, "mom and pop won't open the pool for awhile yet."

"Aw shucks" said Teddi Bear. "I was really hoping to swim since it has been so long since we had a pool to swim in. I missed our pool so much at the other house. I'm glad we have one again here. I can't wait until the pool opens up."

"Me too" said Colby, "but we still have a big yard to play in here, not as big as the other one but it's good for us to play in. There's a garden at the back but I bet mom puts in some more gardens."

Colby and Teddi Bear ran back into the house and skid across the floor in the kitchen. Colby went splat! All four legs out and slid on his belly. Teddi Bear was laughing so hard he was holding his tummy. He went to walk over to Colby and he slid on the floor too. His front legs went flying out from under him and his bum ended up sticking up in the air as he slid. Colby laughed at Teddi Bear. Mom was standing in the kitchen and she was laughing too.

"You must be careful boys. These floors are slippery, even more so when you're wet, but they are also indestructible. You can't scratch them at all. I'll put some mats around the floor so you'll be able to walk without sliding.

We can't play today boys" said mom "I have to unpack and try to get everything set up so you have to stay out of the way." Colby and Teddi Bear slowly walked into the hall trying not to slip and wondering what they could do.

"Let's go upstairs" suggested Teddi Bear. "Okay" agreed Colby. They ran up the stairs, which were carpeted as well as the upstairs where the bedrooms are. They enjoyed running from room to room around the boxes chasing each other.

"Let's go outside to play." said Colby. They went back down to the kitchen and stood in front of the patio doors for mom to let them outside. She did and Colby and Teddi Bear ran to the side of the covered pool.

"I can't wait until they take this cover off so we can swim again" said Teddi Bear. "Hey watch me walk around the pool, on the cover, on my back legs and on my toes!" he said.

"You can't do that!" exclaimed Colby.

"Yes, I can" laughed Teddi Bear, "watch!" And so he stood up on his back legs at the end of the pool and tippy toed slowly around the edge of the pool, keeping his front legs out for balance. Slowly, slowly he went, nearly falling a couple of times. After rounding the end of the pool Teddi Bear started to lose his balance again!

"Whoa, whoa!" he laughed then he toppled right over onto the safety cover and bounced and rolled down into the center of it. Colby was holding his tummy, he was laughing so hard. Colby said "Come on out of there you crazy dog."

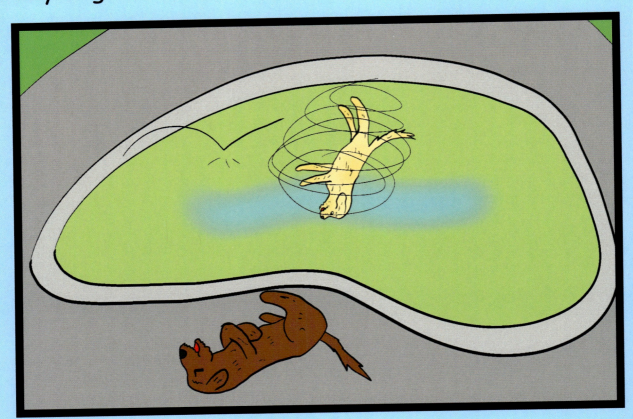

Hey, what's this?" said Colby and he walked to the other side of the pool where the fence was. He bent down and noticed that the fence didn't go right down to the ground. "Hey Teddi come here quick!" Teddi Bear ran to Colby "What do you want" he asked Colby. Look, the fence is about four inches from the ground. If we both dig really fast, we can escape again and go have some fun!"

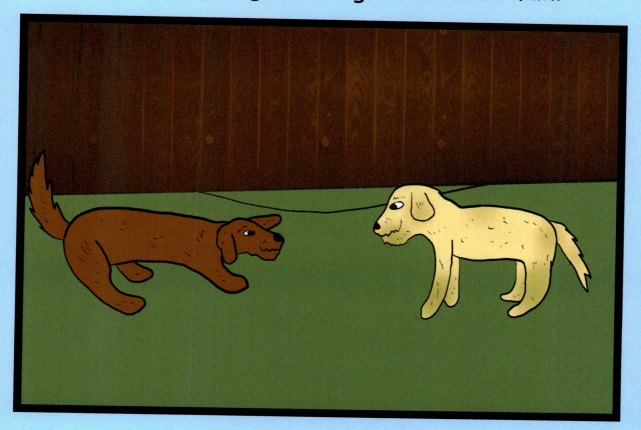

"Okay, I'm good with that," said Teddi Bear. Both Colby and Teddi Bear started digging really fast so mom wouldn't catch them.

"Do you think this is good enough?" Teddi Bear asked Colby. "Let me try" suggested Teddi Bear. He squeezed and kicked but couldn't quite get through. Colby grabbed his legs and pulled him back out. They dug some more, then Teddi Bear tried to get through again and he made it. Then Colby squeezed through. He had a more difficult time because Colby was larger than Teddi Bear so Teddi Bear grabbed Colby's front paws and pulled him. When Colby squeezed through, he made a popping sound (pop)

"Yay" said Colby "and mom didn't see us this time. Now we have to leave here fast because this is the neighbours yard and if they see us they may call mom."

"Hurry, let's go then! said Teddi Bear excitedly. They ran through the neighbours yard, which wasn't fenced and ran down the street on the sidewalk. "Wow! There's lots of cars on this road. Why don't we go down this street and get away from all the traffic" suggested Colby. "Sure" said Teddi Bear.

They walked down the street for a couple of blocks and it was all houses. Suddenly they heard 'clip, clop, clip clop' and turned around real fast. On the road was what they think was called a horse and carriage with two people riding in it.

"Wow! Look how big that horse is!" exclaimed Colby. Teddi Bear started barking right away. He was a bit afraid but Colby told him not to be. "Horses are good Teddi Bear. They're beautiful and big and friendly. Don't bark at the horse Teddi Bear. Let's go see him.

"Oh, Colby do you think we should?" asked Teddi Bear.

"Sure, come on!"

Colby and Teddi Bear slowly walked toward the horse and the man stopped the horse from walking. Colby and Teddi Bear sniffed the horse's nose while the horse sniffed them too. Teddi Bear walked all around the horse and Colby tried to talk to it but it didn't understand him. The horse rubbed Colby's head.

Teddi Bear laughed and said" Maybe he thinks you're a baby horse Colby!"

"Ha, ha!" laughed Colby. I don't think I smell like a horse. I smell like a dog. This horse is really nice. I like him."

"I like him too." Said Teddi Bear. The man clicked his tongue and wiggled his reins on the horses back and the horse started walking down the street again.

"That was exciting" said Teddi Bear as he jumped out of the way.

Come on, let's go and find something else exciting to do
!" said Colby. "Oh look! A great big farmer's field."

"What's a farmer's field?" asked Teddi Bear.

"It's where they grow vegetables" replied Colby.

"Vegetables!" exclaimed Teddi Bear. "Let's go see what
they have in here" said Teddi Bear. Suddenly they saw a
rabbit hopping in the field and started chasing it.

"Why are we chasing the rabbit?" asked Teddi Bear.

"Just for fun" replied Colby. "It's what dogs do!" Off
they went, chasing the rabbit through the farmers field,
zig zagging all over behind the rabbit. Colby stopped so
Teddi Bear did too. "Why are you stopping!" asked Teddi
Bear.

"Whew! I'm out of breath!" replied Colby. "But that was
fun! Let's see what else we can find in the field.

Colby and Teddi Bear walked through the field then spotted a gopher.

"Hey look!" said Teddi Bear, "let's go chase after that one!"

"Don't catch it though, I think it might bite you."

"Why would it bite me?" asked Teddi Bear.

"Because you're chasing it" said Colby "and it will run because it is afraid of you."

"Oh, I don't want to chase it then" said Teddi Bear. "Let's just run around and chase each other then." "Okay, you can't catch me!" said Teddi Bear and he dashed off into the field, zig zagging like the rabbit did. Colby was right behind Teddi Bear but couldn't catch him. It didn't take very long for both of them to get tired again. "Wow" I haven't run like this for a long time. Not since the cottage." "I miss the cottage and the lake" said Teddi Bear. "Me too" commented Colby, "we had a lot of fun there. What do you say we look for some more places around here. See what we can find."

Colby and Teddi Bear walked through the field for a little while. They noticed there were a lot of birds in the field and they would fly off when Colby and Teddi Bear would approach them. Teddi Bear started to chase them just to see them all fly up at the same time. He got tired of doing that after a few minutes then walked with Colby again.

"Sniff, sniff, Colby do you smell that?" asked Teddi Bear.

"Sniff, sniff, yes! Someone is BBQing like pop does. It smells so good and I'm hungry!" exclaimed Colby.

"Do you think we can sneak up and grab some food?" asked Teddi Bear.

"We can try!" laughed Colby. They got low in the grass and wriggled their way toward the man who was BBQing.

"Oh, it smells so good!" exclaimed Colby. He was fairly drooling as he was crawling. When they got close, Colby told Teddi Bear to wait and see if the man left the BBQ so they could quickly grab something off it.

A cat walked through the grass and sniffed them from a distance, wondering what they were doing there.

"Stay" said Teddi Bear "and we will share with you. Oh, the man is going into the house now. Come on Colby, let's go!"

Teddi Bear and Colby ran toward the BBQ. They stayed on the side and Colby quickly pulled down a couple of steaks because they were hot.

"Wait a minute Teddi Bear, They're hot."

"We have to go Colby, the man is going to come back!" said Teddi Bear.

"Okay, grab one and let's go."

They both grabbed a steak carefully and ran to the spot where they were before. The cat was still there, with a goofy smile on his face and Colby bit off a piece of his steak and gave it to him. All three ate their steaks while keeping an ear out for the man. They heard him come back outside then he exclaimed "Hey! What happened to the steaks? Where did they go?" He looked around the house and garage but couldn't find anything or anyone who could have taken them. He looked up in the sky just in case a big bird could have flown over and taken them. He was very puzzled. The two dogs and the cat had finished the yummy steaks but kept lying low in the tall grasses so they wouldn't be seen.

"Wait until he goes back in the house then we can run away." The man went back into the house as Colby was saying that and away they ran with the cat following them.

Next, they came upon a farm. This farm grew apples and vegetables. Colby didn't like apples but Teddi Bear loved them and began eating the apples on the ground. He let the cat lick the juices off the apple pieces.

"Look Teddi Bear, there's some people picking apples a couple of rows over." "Oh! Neat!" exclaimed Teddi Bear. They watched the people pick apples for a few minutes then decided to leave to see what else they could discover.

They walked for about fifteen minutes through the trees then came upon rows and rows of vegetables. Colby said

"I don't like vegetables either." Teddi Bear said.

"You like sweet potatoes so why don't we see if they have any here?"

"Okay let's look!" said Colby.

The three of them walked through the rows of vegetables until finally Teddi Bear said,

"Here we go! Rows and rows of sweet potato leaves. We have to dig them up though."

The dogs started digging up the sweet potatoes.

"Yum, these are good," said Colby. " Just brush the dirt off them."

The cat licked a piece of sweet potato but he didn't like it too much. He just sat beside the dogs until they were finished eating.

"Whew! I'm full now" said Teddi Bear. "I've had steak, apples and sweet potatoes. That's a good diet for today!" "Lets go check out that big red building over there!" said Teddi Bear. That's where I live "said the cat.

"Really!" exclaimed Colby, "that's a big house!"

"That's a barn silly!" said the cat. "Cows and horses and chickens live in there! They all come out in the daytime and go where they want in the fenced areas. They eat grass and seed!"

"I have fun in there because I can climb to the top of the rafters and watch everyone."

"Can we go to the rafters too?" asked Teddi Bear.

"If you can climb a ladder, you can." replied the cat

"We used to climb the ladder to get out of the pool before the steps were put in" said Teddi Bear.

"Well then you may be able to climb this ladder then, although it is much longer." the cat said.

"Let's try then" said Teddi Bear. All three walked into the barn and when they saw how high the ladder was, Colby said,

"Ohh dear" Teddi Bear said,

"I don't know about this."

"Why not?" asked Colby "you climbed ladders when we went to the circus."

"Yes, but that seemed different. Let's try them" said Teddi Bear."

"Okay" agreed Colby.

"Oh Colby, I'm scared!" exclaimed Teddi Bear.

"It's okay Teddi Bear", said Colby, "keep going, you're doing okay. Just remember the pool ladder and look up to where you want to go." Teddi Bear looked up to the platform and scrambled up the rest of the way.

"Whew!" Teddi Bear said, "I made it! This isn't so bad afterall! Come on Colby!" The cat ran up the ladder and Colby went up after him.

Soon all three were standing on the loft looking out the window over the pastures. "This is wonderful!" said Colby, "just one problem. We never climbed down the ladder to get into the pool. We always jumped in!"

"Oh, oh" said Teddi Bear" we're in trouble now!"

"No you're not "said the cat, "you just reverse your steps to go down. I can go down head first but I have sharp claws and won't fall. Let's get comfortable up here and watch the barn animals for awhile." They watched the barn animals for awhile and all three fell asleep in the hay on the loft.

After awhile Colby slowly woke up and was alarmed immediately. "Hey guys wake up, wake up! It's dark outside! There's only a little light on down in the barn! We have to get home! Mom and pop will be so worried about us.

"We can't go down the ladder in the dark!" exclaimed Teddi Bear, and I don't want to walk home in the dark either!"

"Don't worry Teddi Bear, we'll stay here tonight and go home in the morning. We've had enough to eat today. Sure could use a drink of water though. We'll get that in the morning too! The two dogs and the one cat sat looking out the barn window watching the last of the sunset and the moon and stars come out.

"This sure is beautiful" remarked Colby. "Sure is" the other two agreed.

Eventually the dogs and cat curled up together in the loft by the window and went to sleep. A couple of birds slept with them too

In the morning Colby, Teddi Bear and Snooker the cat all climbed very carefully down the ladder. Snooker showed them how to go down backwards. It was kind of scary but kind of fun too.

"Hey Snooker, why don't you come home with us, then you'll know where we live and can come visit and play?" asked Teddi Bear, "do you like swimming because we have a pool we swim in all the time!"

"No, I think I'll pass on the pool. Cat's don't like water and don't swim." replied Snooker, "but I can sit in the warm sun and watch you guys." "Okay, let's go home. We won't be able to play today because we're going to be in big trouble for leaving again. The boys walked back through the farmers fields, spotting a few rabbits and birds along the way. Teddi Bear would chase the birds and Snooker would chase the rabbits and Colby would call them back.

When they arrived at the fence they couldn't get back under, the hole had been filled in. So, Colby and Teddi Bear walked to the front door with Snooker.

"This is where we live Snooker. Come back in a few days and we'll be able to play. Thank you for everything on our adventure!: Teddy Bear exclaimed.

"Nice meeting you guys," said Snooker, "see you soon." Snooker left toward the fields and Colby and Teddi Bear started barking at the door. In a minute the door flung open and mom was crying, she was so happy to see the dogs back.

73

"Where have you been? Pop is still looking for you! I'll have to call him to let him know you are home! I'm so happy you're home but you are still naughty dogs for leaving! Pop and I were worried sick about you. We will have to make sure you can't dig any more holes under the fence so you can't get away. Now go to your beds!"

"Wow, mom sure was mad at us. Whew we should just go to our beds like she said."

Colby and Teddi Bear weren't allowed out for a few days except to do their business then they had to go right in. Colby and Teddi Bear would spend their days lying by the patio doors looking outside wishing they could go out there. Finally, mom let them out with a stern warning not to dig under the fence. While they had been stuck inside, pop had put big rocks all along the fence so the dogs couldn't get out. They hoped. Colby and Teddi Bear didn't mind the rocks, they knew their friend could still get into the yard and hoped to see him soon. In the meantime, Colby and Teddi Bear played in the pool and would lie in the sun to dry off. Sometimes mom and pop would play with them with their balls and pool toys.

One day Colby and Teddi Bear were lying beside the pool when they heard a quiet meow from the top of the fence.

"Snooker!" Colby exclaimed, "so good to see you! Come on down!" Teddi Bear ran to him and nudged his nose a couple of times.

"Hi guys! How are you?" asked Snooker the cat.

"We're great now that you're here" said Colby.

"Come play with us in the pool!" exclaimed Teddi Bear.

"No, I don't like water remember" said Snooker.

"I have an idea. You could go on this floaty thing and we could push you around! But don't put your claws into it because it will break and our mom and pop will be mad at us again." suggested Colby.

"Okay I'll try that but don't tip me over!" Snooker gingerly stepped onto the floaty, remembering not to put his claws out. Colby and Teddi Bear slowly pushed him around the pool. Mom saw them and called pop. "Do you believe this?", she asked pop, "they must have made friends with the cat when they were gone! I've never seen something like this before. Our dogs may be mischievous but they sure are smart."

"They certainly are.", said pop. Mom and pop stayed at the patio doors watching the dogs and cat play in the pool. All of a sudden Colby sneezed hard and tipped the floaty down making the cat fall off into the water. The cat started to snort and choke on the water then suddenly started to swim to the edge of the pool.

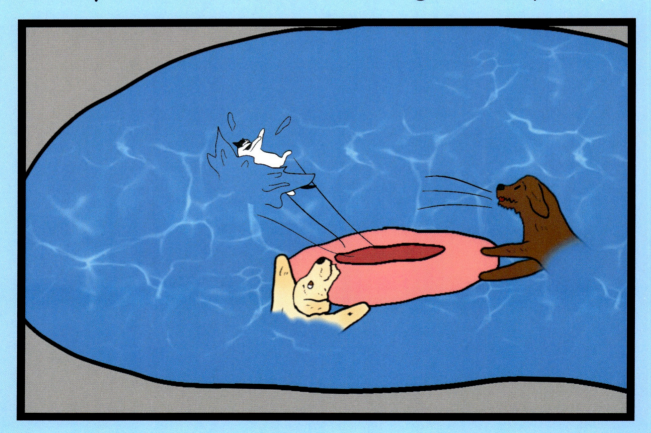

"Snooker, get on my back "yelled Colby. Colby swam right next to Snooker and he climbed onto the back of Colby's neck. Colby swam to the stairs and climbed out of the water. Snooker jumped off Colby, spotted a nice lounge chair and jumped up on that. He began licking all the water off his fur. Teddi Bear and Colby shook themselves then lay down beside the lounger and soon they were all napping in the sun.

Oh! Those crazy dogs!

Books in the "Oh Those Crazy Dogs" Series by author **CAL**

Book one	Colby Comes Home
Book two	Teddi Bear Comes Home
Book three	Teddi Bear's First Time at the Lake!
Book four	A New Friend In The Neighbourhood! DIGGER!
Book five	Teddi Bear and Colby Love Swimming in the Pool
Book six	Colby and Teddi Bear Go To The Circus
Book seven	Tyse Comes To Visit
Book eight	Winter Fun
Book nine	Fun At The Cottage – Winter and Summer
Book ten	We're Moving!
Book eleven	Colby and Teddi Bear Move Again

Printed in the United States
by Baker & Taylor Publisher Services